About the Author

Matthew Flax has been obsessed with storytelling since an early age. He spent many a dreary school day lost in a fantasy world. He studied film at the University of Cape Town and graduated with honours in 2007. He has worked as a travel writer, and freelanced for various digital marketing agencies. His work is the product of an alacritous and occasionally unhinged mind.

Tales from the Valley of Whispers

Matthew Flax

Tales from the Valley of Whispers

Vanguard Press

VANGUARD PAPERBACK

© Copyright 2024
Matthew Flax

The right of Matthew Flax to be identified as author of this work has been asserted by him in accordance with the Copyright, Designs and Patents Act 1988.

All Rights Reserved

No reproduction, copy or transmission of this publication may be made without written permission.
No paragraph of this publication may be reproduced, copied or transmitted save with the written permission of the publisher, or in accordance with the provisions of the Copyright Act 1956 (as amended).

Any person who commits any unauthorised act in relation to this publication may be liable to criminal prosecution and civil claims for damages.

A CIP catalogue record for this title is available from the British Library.

ISBN 978-1-83794-257-2

This is a work of fiction. Names, characters, businesses, places, events and incidents are either the products of the author's imagination or used in a fictitious manner. Any resemblance to actual persons, living or dead, or actual events is purely coincidental.

Vanguard Press is an imprint of
Pegasus Elliot Mackenzie Publishers Ltd.
www.pegasuspublishers.com

First Published in 2024

Vanguard Press
Sheraton House Castle Park
Cambridge England

Printed & Bound in Great Britain

Where was the hand to take my hand
When I could not open my eyes?
Where was the voice to tell me truth
When the voices all told lies?
It was so cold, for so long.
All the places that I've been
In a mind that's torn and broken
By all the visions that I've seen.

The Old Man in the Cave

His eyes fluttered open. Light trickled into the cave from beyond the white sky.

The old man who had forgotten his own name crept slowly towards the edge of the cliff, keeping the blankets wrapped tightly around himself to guard against the cold. He gazed out upon the valley below.

A carpet of green forest stretched from the foot of the mountain, as far as the eye could see. It was beautiful to look upon, but he knew what dread the forest concealed. The howl of the wind against the mountainside made him shiver.

His morning routine began with him carrying a clay pot down the rock path to a small waterfall. He bathed in the rock pool for a short while; the cold water helping to awaken his senses. Once he was done, he filled the pot with water and returned to the cave, where he started a fire and placed the pot above it.

As he waited for the water to boil, he took a handful of berries from a basket at the edge of the cave. He noted that the basket was almost empty, and resolved to venture into the forest later to gather more berries. This would give him a chance to check the traps. If he was lucky, he would have rabbit for dinner, and berries for breakfast tomorrow.

He poured some of the boiled water into a beaten old cup and went to sit at the edge of the cliff outside the cave mouth. He would wait for the sun to rise higher in the sky before heading for the forest; there was little enough light and warmth in there as it was. In the meantime, he sat with his cup and felt grateful for the sense of peace. He had been fortunate to find this place.

He remembered how terrified he had been to leave the cave when he first discovered it. He would cower against the walls, expecting a shadow to cross the entrance at any moment.

He had gone for days without eating, and only rainwater to drink.

Eventually, starvation forced him out into the open. He had relied on berries to start, slowly working up the courage to try and set traps. Over time, he grew in confidence. He realised he had found one of the few havens in the valley that the denizens of the forest seemed unaware of.

I've come a long way since then, he thought to himself. He looked up at the sky; the sun was high enough to make an excursion into the forest a realistic prospect.

He made his way back down the path, passing by the rock pool. A field of grass stretched out before him, ending at a wall of trees that marked the boundary of the forest; the edge of the known world as far as he was concerned.

He stood there for a few moments, bracing himself. Then he took a deep breath, and made his way towards the wall of trees, passing through them into the darkness beyond.

It was a different world within the forest. The canopy above allowed only a little light to filter through, making it a place of shadows and silence.

He moved quietly, sensitive to any sound. Any berries and edible plants he could find were placed in a leather sack slung over his shoulder, along with sticks that he could use for a fire. He checked the traps and was elated to find a caught rabbit, which he tied to his belt. The rest of his excursion passed without incident, and he felt a sense of relief as he left the forest and returned to the cave.

Night fell; the light from the fire reflected on his face, and the wind howled against the mountainside; but he sat warm and safe, watching the rabbit cook in the pot. He ate well that night.

It was three days before he felt the need to venture into the forest again, but this time it would not go as planned.

As he crept through the maze of trees, he saw something that caused him to freeze and drop the pile of firewood he was carrying. There was a body lying on the ground, completely still.

Oh no, he thought. *Please, no.*

He approached the body slowly, heart thumping in his chest. As he came closer, he saw that it was a woman, her head turned to one side, facing away from him. The cloth she wore was torn in places, most likely where it had snagged on branches as she ran. There was no sign of injury, but she was dead.

He scanned the surroundings for any threat, then crouched beside her and gently turned her head. Upon seeing her face, he gasped and lunged backwards. Her eyes were completely white.

He scurried to his feet, turned, and ran as fast as a man of his years could. He burst through the wall of trees and out into the light, giving no thought to anything other than the need to reach the cave. He limped up the rock path, arrived at the entrance to the cave and fell to the ground, gasping for breath.

Night came, but he would light no fire this time, nor eat any rabbit stew. He crawled deep into the cave until he was right up against the rock, and wrapped himself in the blanket, trembling. Thoughts were racing through his head. Was he still safe? Should he leave? How long would it be before he found shelter again?

Eventually, exhaustion won out, and he drifted into a troubled sleep, but his respite wouldn't last long.

Deep into the night, he awoke, and immediately felt that something was wrong.

There was something at the entrance to the cave, he sensed its presence.

He shut his eyes tightly, afraid to breathe. He didn't dare look or make any movement at all. That which stood at the entrance to the cave didn't move either, but he knew it was watching.

They've found me. The thought kept repeating in his head. *They've finally found me.* He felt the familiar sense of dread.

Then he heard it. The whispers, faint to begin with, but gradually rising in strength, echoing through the cave. The intruder remained at the entrance, but the whispers were coming from everywhere. For what seemed like hours on end, he lay there, clutching at the blanket, waiting for death to come.

But then the whispers stopped. The creature remained at the entrance for a moment longer, silently watching. Then it was gone.

The old man lay still, wrapped tightly in the blanket, trembling in fear. He listened for the sound of whispers, certain they would return at any moment, that he would look up to see the creature looming above him. But the night passed, and the creature did not return.

The next morning, he awoke, still alive, but no longer safe. He tossed what few belongings he had into the leather sack; the clay pot, the old basket with some berries in it, a small knife made of bone, the tin cup, and the blanket. He didn't bother with any of the firewood; he would not be lighting any fires out there.

He took one last look at the cave that had been his sanctuary for so long and headed out into the wilderness. He stopped at the rock pool to drink some water, and fill a leather skin that he had tied to his belt. Then, he entered the forest again.

He avoided venturing in too deep. So long as he stuck to the outskirts and kept the mountainside in his sight, he could avoid getting lost. There was always a chance he would stumble upon another cave, although he would need to travel for at least five days before he could be sure that he had made enough distance.

He travelled for a while. As darkness approached, he looked for a place to bed down for the night. He saw a cluster of rocks a short distance from the edge of the forest. They would hopefully conceal him from sight.

As he settled down amidst the rocks, he took a swig from his waterskin and munched on some berries. As unnatural as this valley seemed; there was still rain, and plants still grew; else he would have died of thirst or starvation ages ago.

He lay down, hoping the rocks would keep him hidden from anything roaming the forest. As sleep took him, he dreamed a strange dream.

He found himself in a cavern, much larger than the cave he had been living in. He couldn't see an entrance, but he could hear the sound of running water, and somehow he knew this place was safe. There was someone here, sitting on a flat rock in the centre of the cavern.

He approached the stranger; the first human being that he had seen in a long time. As he drew closer, he saw that it was a man, dressed in a cloth robe, sitting upon the rock in a meditative pose with legs crossed and eyes closed. He radiated an aura of peace, and though he was seated in the centre of the cavern, it felt like he was everywhere at once.

The man's eyes flitted open and turned to look at the old man. He didn't seem surprised to see him. He simply smiled and nodded reassuringly. Then he closed his eyes again.

The old man felt himself drifting away. He wanted to stay here, but he was being pulled back to his body. He awoke, back in the valley where every day was a struggle to survive, where each day could be his last.

The dream hadn't lasted that long, yet it was already morning here. He sat up and packed the blanket into his sack. The image of the stranger from his dream was still with him.

Although he feared what lay ahead, he felt new strength coursing through him. He couldn't be certain that the dream was real, but the belief that it was gave him comfort. Perhaps, the cave from his dream truly existed, somewhere in this valley. Perhaps, if he survived long enough, he would find it. Somehow, he knew that if he did, his struggle, at last, would be over.

He munched on some berries, took a swig from his waterskin and headed back into the forest.

The Village at the Edge of Night

At the foot of the mountains that surround the valley lay a small village, a village that had never known daylight.

The village was surrounded by glittering torches on one side, and mountains on the other. Beyond the lights cast by the torches lay the darkness of the forest, where none dared venture.

A lone figure stood on the edge of the torchlight, gazing out into the darkness beyond. He stretched out his arms, bathing in the strange energy emitted by the torches.

No one knew what this energy was, or how it was created; all they knew was that it kept whatever lurked in the forest at bay.

The lone figure was a young man, no older than twenty-five, and the elders of the village did not like it when he did this. But Thobi would do it anyway, more often than he should.

The torches glittered in the darkness, Thobi dared himself to step beyond them. The elders had warned against doing so, as no one that had left the boundaries of the village ever returned.

This would not be the night he tested fate. Instead, he turned and headed back towards the cluster of stone huts that formed the village—the only home he had ever known.

"You know old Aada doesn't like it when you do that?" said a child's voice.

Thobi stopped and turned to see little Elea standing beside one of the huts. She was no more than ten years of age, but her sharp eyes never seemed to miss anything.

"I've been made aware of that, many times," he said with a wry grin.

Elea didn't return the smile. None of his friends were happy about him taking such risks.

"You've been summoned to the gathering hut. Aada wants to speak with you," said Elea.

Thobi sighed. That was never a good thing.

"Well, see you soon, I hope," he said, and headed off in the direction of old Aada's hut.

Elea watched him go, and the tiniest of smiles touched the corners of her lips.

A fireplace illuminated the gathering hut, where a circle of elders sat cross-legged on the ground. Aada sat at the head of the circle; her milky white eyes fixed on the centre. She always seemed to be staring at something that no one else could see.

She was a woman of about seventy, with long, dishevelled grey hair and a wrinkled face. She didn't look up as Thobi entered the hut.

"Ah, the brave one graces us with his presence," she said. The shadows cast by the fire danced across her face.

Thobi feigned confusion, but it was no use. Aada knew where he had been.

"Do you think it wise," she continued, "to endanger the village as you do, just to satisfy your own childish curiosity? Do you think that… what's out there… does not see you?"

Thobi remained silent.

"You draw their attention to us. I can't have that."

She finally raised her head and looked up at him. "Is that understood?"

Thobi nodded. Aada held him with her eyes for a few moments, then turned her attention back to whatever lay in the centre of the circle.

Thobi looked around the hut. There were murals on the walls; one of them depicted a frightening, shadowy creature with tendrils reaching out to ensnare what looked like a female child. He turned away from the disturbing image.

The elders were all staring into space, as though they feared witnessing the exchange would offend Aada. All but one of them, Rodrik, who gave Thobi an encouraging smile.

"The barrier is weakening. There will be another sacrifice," said Aada.

Thobi's heart sank.

"Who will it be?" he asked quietly.

"That is yet to be revealed. What is known is that you will be the one to perform it."

No, it can't be, he thought.

No one as young as him had ever been called to perform a sacrifice, but it was no use pointing that out. Aada's only response would be an empty, uncaring gaze.

"I volunteer myself as the sacrifice," he finally said.

He had promised himself that if he was ever called on to perform a sacrifice, he would volunteer himself instead. Others before him had done the same.

He hadn't expected to face such a choice so soon, though.

"No," said Aada, "you are too old. The Protector demands a younger sacrifice. It will be a child."

"What? That can't be!" he blurted out.

Aada slowly turned towards him. Again, he felt her ghostly eyes piercing through him.

"This is what the dreams have shown me. It is not our choice to make."

Thobi looked pleadingly at the circle of elders, but none of them would meet his eyes, not even Rodrik.

"Go now, and prepare for the task ahead," said Aada, as though she were instructing him to fetch water. "It will take place within the week."

He followed the pathway, illuminated by a row of torches on each side, as with all pathways in the village, to the hut he shared with other young men. His mind was racing, and the confusion must have shown on his face, judging from the occasional questioning glances he received from the others as they went about their tasks.

Julien entered the hut. Thobi and Julien were close, yet he was reluctant to tell him about Aada's command.

Nonetheless, Julien clearly sensed something was wrong. He came up and put a hand on Thobi's shoulder.

"Are you all right? You look pale."

Thobi forced a smile. "Aada told me off for approaching the barrier again."

"As she should. It's not wise."

Thobi shrugged. "I've done it plenty of times, nothing's ever happened."

"That's what the barrier's for," said Julien, "but one of these days you're going to push it too far. I worry for you."

"The barrier protects the village."

"I don't care about the village. I care about you."

Thobi just shrugged.

He kept his mind occupied with various chores. Sometime later, he heard the sound of drums. It was the signal for villagers to gather in the square; three beats of the drum meant it was mealtime.

As he left the hut, he saw the villager with the drum pass by. The duty of summoning villagers was rotated; Thobi himself had done it many times, going from hut to hut banging gently on the drum. There was something solemn about the whole process.

He arrived at the village square. A steaming cauldron of porridge sat above a fire pit in the centre; villagers with wooden bowls were approaching it one by one. A female elder stood beside the cauldron and dished out two spoonsful of porridge to each villager.

Thobi joined the queue, bowl in hand. He saw Rodrik and one of the other elders leave Aada's hut and approach the cauldron. Rodrik held out a large wooden bowl, and the woman dished four spoonsful into it. Rodrik thanked her, turned and headed back to the hut; followed by the other elder. At the entrance to the hut, he stopped to look around, and saw Thobi watching him. He gave a quick nod before disappearing into the hut.

Thobi finished his porridge. It was the third meal of the daily cycle; the final meal before sleep, but there was still some time before curfew. He sought out Rodrik, who should have been finished with Aada by now.

He found him in his hut, sitting on the edge of his mattress and scrubbing dirt off his boots. The elders were each assigned their own hut as a mark of their station.

"Has the sacrifice ever required a child before?" Thobi asked.

"No... it hasn't. Not for as long as I can remember," said Rodrik.

"Why would the Protector want this?"

"Only Aada receives the commands of the Protector; and she only tells us the what, not the why. You know this as well as I do."

"Maybe it's time we asked why."

Rodrik flinched, as though someone had struck him. "Careful, Thobias. Aada may be the only one the Protector speaks to, but she's not the only one he hears."

Thobi believed he could trust Rodrik, but he also knew Rodrik was afraid, just like everyone else in the village.

"I've wondered about that."

Rodrik looked up sharply. "What do you mean?"

Sometimes, when Thobi was alone, he'd say things about Aada he would never say to her face. Not because he resented her, but because he wanted to see if she would find out. He wanted to see if the Protector would warn her in her visions. But as far as he could tell, that never happened.

"I speak to him sometimes, just to see if he hears me. I say things I probably shouldn't."

"I would advise against that."

"Aada's never said anything to me about it. Maybe the Protector never told her."

"Maybe he did. Maybe this is your punishment." Rodrik turned his attention back to his shoes, scrubbing them hard with the cloth.

Thobi was getting frustrated. He knew he shouldn't say what he was about to say.

"Was it punishment when Aada made you sacrifice Vilmer?"

Rodrik froze. He and Vilmer had been close, and being close to anyone in that way was not encouraged. If it was time for a child to be made, Aada would choose a man and woman from the village to perform the necessary act. The Protector supposedly knew which couplings would produce strong children.

None of the young men or women of the village were ever told who their birth parents were. Their loyalty must be to the village, and the Protector. They lived because the Protector watched over them, and that was all they needed to know. So said Aada.

"It was for the good of the village," Rodrik said, quietly. "I didn't question it, and neither should you. The sacrifices preserve the barrier."

There was nothing more to be said. Thobi turned and left.

Julien was waiting at their usual spot. He put an arm around Thobi's shoulders.

"You still look troubled," he said, "Aada must have had harsh words for you."

"Does she ever have kind words?"

"Maybe she would if you stopped playing with the barrier. There's nothing but night beyond."

"Maybe there's something beyond the night."

Julien's expression turned grim. "You wouldn't live long enough to find out."

People won't live long in the village either if we start sacrificing children, thought Thobi. The two of them sat in silence for a while, staring out into the darkness. It was a brief escape from the grim responsibility that now faced him; all too brief, for curfew came and they returned to the sleeping hut.

Thobi had a dream that night; a dream he had many times before.

He was surrounded by trees; there was something bright above them. It cast a light, different from the light created by fire. This light was everywhere. He believed the bright object above the trees was what they called the sun.

The forest canopy was all-encompassing, but the light was powerful enough to penetrate it. He reached out to touch a ray of light; it felt warm and comforting. He felt strength surging through his body, and his mind. Deep down, he knew that this was how people were meant to live, not in darkness, but in light.

But suddenly, everything went still. Thobi froze. He realised there was something different about the dream this time. There was someone else here.

The ray of light disappeared. His hands went cold. Darkness passed overhead and blotted out the sun. The trees closed in around him. There was a presence here, and that presence meant him harm.

Then, he heard the whispers.

They started off faint, but grew louder, coming from all directions. He looked around desperately, trying to find the source of the whispers. A cold wind blew through the trees, piercing his tunic; and shadowy creatures appeared in the distance.

Suddenly, the whispers ceased, and a voice rang out through the forest.

"So this is the one."

Thobi felt overwhelming dread. He turned slowly in the direction of the voice.

And there it was; a figure resembling a man but cloaked completely in darkness. It wore robes that stretched out around it like tendrils, and its features were concealed by shadows, but Thobi felt its eyes upon him.

"I will tear him apart," the voice said. As the stranger spoke, Thobi could hear screams in the distance; the sound of many people crying out in agony and despair.

"I will rip out his heart and feed it to the shadows," the voice continued, "and then I will twist and torture his soul. He will know pain beyond comprehension, and it will be your doing."

The figure began moving towards him with inhuman speed, gliding over the ground like a cloak caught in the wind. Thobi backed away, scanning the forest for an escape route but seeing only shadows closing in around him.

He awoke, trembling.

The dreams of the forest usually left him with a sense of peace, but this time, he was overcome with dread. His body was tensed up as though someone was about to cut his stomach open.

The terror slowly faded, replaced by a persistent fear. Eventually, he drifted off into a fitful sleep.

Hours later, the sound of the drums signalled the first meal of the daily cycle. Thobi stepped out into the night and made for the village square. His hands trembled as he held out his bowl to receive two spoonsful of porridge.

Again, two elders emerged from Aada's hut and approached the cauldron. Four spoonsful were dished into Aada's bowl, and they took it back to her hut.

Thobi finished his porridge and was about to leave the square when the two elders reemerged and headed straight for him.

"You've been summoned," one of them said.

Thobi's nerves had finally begun to settle, but now he felt fear bubble up in his stomach again. He followed the elders back to Aada's hut.

Aada sat cross-legged on the floor, with an elder on either side of her. She made sucking noises as she spooned the last few bits of porridge into her mouth, then wiped her lips on her sleeve. She held up the empty bowl. One of the elders took it and left the hut.

She looked up at Thobi, her eyes tinged with suspicion.

"The sacrifice has been moved forward," she said, "it will take place after the third meal."

Thobi was aghast.

"Why?" he asked. Aada glared at him icily.

"It will take place after the third meal," she repeated, "and a child has been chosen. Go now and prepare yourself in whatever way you see fit."

Thobi returned to the sleeping hut. He lay on the straw mattress, unsure what to do. His mind was racing, desperately seeking a way out. He stared at the flickering lights of the torches that lined the walls.

Who had been chosen for the sacrifice? Would it be Elea? He was certain it would be. He was clearly being subjected to some form of punishment, so it was likely someone close to him would be chosen.

The second meal of the cycle came and went. Thobi was still lying on the mattress. Julien came to find out why he hadn't attended the meal. He was shocked to see Thobi in such a state, and immediately went to fetch an elder, but he came back alone, his face pale. He sat silently at Thobi's bedside for a while, then left.

The third meal arrived. Thobi had been tossing and turning for hours on end, but he forced himself to rise and head for the square. Villagers were milling about, attending to their own business. Javik, one of the other young men in the village, was sitting on a rock, staring into space. Thobi envied him.

There were barrels containing water on the edge of the square. Thobi approached them and splashed some water on his face. One of the elders was there, filling his bowl. He noticed Thobi, and shuffled away nervously.

Now was the time to make a run for it, but that wouldn't stop the sacrifice. Someone else would be chosen to perform it, and a child would die.

Thobi knew what he had to do.

He returned to the hut. Soon enough, a group of elders came to fetch him.

They took him to a cave at the foot of the mountain. Thobi remembered the cave. People of the village had played near the entrance as children, daring each other to go in. No one ever did.

Something felt wrong about the cave. It felt wrong when they were children, and it felt wrong now. Finally, he knew why.

They entered the cave. The elders of the village were standing around a stone altar in the centre. They were holding torches. Shadows danced across the stone walls.

Rodrik was with them, but his eyes were fixed firmly on the altar. He didn't look up as Thobi entered. Aada was not in attendance. That was no surprise to Thobi, nor was he surprised to see Elea lying face-up on the altar.

She was staring up at the ceiling, seemingly unaware of her surroundings. It was all the more painful to see her like this; her eyes devoid of their usual spark.

One of the elders approached him. "She has been given something for the pain," he said. "She won't feel a thing." He handed Thobi a knife. It was made of a substance he had never felt before; something that glittered in the torchlight like water yet was near as sturdy as stone.

The elders parted to create a space at the head of the altar and beckoned him forward. He approached, clutching the hilt of the knife tightly.

The elder who had handed him the knife spoke again. "Plunge the blade into her heart, it will be quick."

Thobi brushed his hand through Elea's hair; she didn't respond to his touch.

Then he lifted her by her shoulders so that she was in a sitting position, wrapped an arm around her, and picked her up.

There was an intake of breath among the elders.

Thobi backed away from the altar and held the knife out in front of him.

"I won't do it," he said.

Two of the elders moved towards him. Rodrik was staring wide-eyed. "Thobi, please…" he said.

But Thobi continued to back away, towards the cave entrance. He swiped at one of the approaching elders, who staggered backwards. Another elder tried to grab him. Thobi lashed out again with the knife, and the elder leapt away, clutching his hand.

More elders approached him, circling around to cut off his escape.

Then something incredible happened.

The chief elder opened his mouth to speak, but froze, as though a cloth had been stuffed down his throat. His eyes widened.

He dropped to his knees. The other elders turned to look at him, confused.

Then the chief elder's eyes lit up with a bright yellow glow. It reminded Thobi of the sunlight he had seen in his dream.

The elder looked up, his face wracked by spasms. A beam of light burst forth from his mouth towards the ceiling. He was frozen, arms outstretched.

One of the other elders moved towards him, only to fall to his knees as well. The same light burst forth from his eyes and mouth. All around the cave, elders were crumbling to the ground, pierced by light.

Rodrik was bewildered. He looked at Thobi. "What are you... what..." Then he fell forward, as though prostrated in prayer. He looked up, his face contorting. His lips moved but no sound came out. Another elder tried to grab Thobi, only to suffer the same fate as the rest. Thobi shielded his eyes as the light burst forth.

Now every elder was in the same pose; paralysed; impaled on beams of light.

Thobi looked around at the stricken elders in awe. Elea's head was resting on his shoulder.

Then Rodrik turned slowly towards him, but it wasn't Rodrik. There was some other presence behind those eyes.

"Run," he said. It was not his voice, and it echoed throughout the cave.

Thobi didn't think twice. He turned, ran towards the cave entrance and out into the silent night. The village was asleep. No one was there to stop him as he made for the boundary.

He halted at the edge of the torchlight, wrapping both arms around Elea as he gazed out towards the dark forest. He had stood here many times before, but something had always held him back. Now, something was urging him on.

He stepped through the barrier, feeling its energy coursing through him.

He was there. He was on the other side.

He took one last glance at the village, and headed towards the forest, passing through the trees and into the unknown.

A Place of Peace

In the depths of the forest, a woman weaved her way amidst the trees, alone.

It had been days since Tara ventured into the forest. She had kept moving, rarely stopping to rest. Her only hope of survival was to stay on the move.

But she was exhausted, and her legs ached. She leaned against a tree, struggling to catch her breath as she scanned her surroundings. Every now and then she thought she caught a glimpse of something lurking in the dark.

She resumed her journey. She was young and strong, and her body could endure much strain, but her mind was on the verge of shattering. She had known nothing but fear for such a long time, that she had forgotten what it was like to feel anything else.

There were shadows in her mind, every bit as terrifying as the ones that lurked in the forest.

The whispers came and went. Sometimes, she felt tempted to surrender to them. It was so hard to keep going, but some part of her still clung to hope; the hope that the stories were true, and that somewhere in the depths of this forest there was a place of peace.

There was no light here. The trees were tall and menacing, with thick, twisted branches that concealed the sky from view.

Even if she found the place she was looking for, would she feel safe again? What if her time in the valley had broken her mind; made it impossible to ever heal?

The whispers faded, but she kept going. It was not time to rest yet. She had to make as much distance as possible.

Night came. It was dark in the forest even during the day; at night the darkness was impenetrable.

She looked for a tree that had a thick enough tangle of branches to hold her weight. The trees here were lifeless, but their branches stretched desperately towards the sky, forming a tangled web just below the canopy.

She climbed up and lay down on one of the outstretched branches, drifting off into a light sleep.

She awoke the next morning to see a hint of sunlight beyond the canopy. Up here in the treetops, it was possible to catch the occasional glimpse of the world above.

But once she returned to the ground, she was again enclosed in darkness.

She resumed her journey, stumbling through the forest as she fought fear and exhaustion. The hardest part was convincing herself there was a reason to go on. Why not just fall to the ground and surrender to the encroaching shadows?

She was sinking deeper into dark thoughts when a burst of light suddenly penetrated the canopy. She looked up in shock, feeling a warmth she had not known in years.

But then the whispers returned.

She lunged forward, forcing herself to pick up the pace. The whispers were growing louder; thoughts of surrender disappeared from her mind and survival instinct kicked in. Part of her wanted to live after all.

There never had been nor ever would be anything else in the world but the whispers. That's what her mind was telling her, but she kept going. She turned and saw something behind her, a creature cloaked in shadows.

The whispers stopped, replaced by a screech of anger and pain that pierced her mind. The shadow closed in on her, gliding effortlessly across the forest floor. She crashed through the underbrush. Terror infused her limbs with newfound strength.

The darkness began to part before her like smoke. Another glance behind; the creature was still in pursuit, almost looming over her as it closed in.

But then she saw something, a bright light shining through the trees.

The screech penetrated her mind yet again, and the shadows reached out like tendrils to enclose her.

Then she burst through the trees and into a clearing.

She was bathed in light; so much light that it felt like she could reach out and touch it. In the centre of the clearing was a tree, larger than any she had ever seen, with lush green leaves brimming with life.

The creature that had been behind her only a moment before was gone, and the only sound she could hear was that of a gentle breeze rustling through the trees.

She collapsed in the shade of the tree. She lay there for a long time, drifting off into a blissful sleep.

When she awoke, night had fallen, but it was a tranquil night, not like the suffocating darkness of the forest. She rolled onto her back and gazed up at the myriad of stars. Tears came to her eyes.

She stood up and walked around the clearing. There was a rock pool, filled with crystal clear water that reflected the moonlight. She drank from it, and then returned to the tree. She took a plump piece of fruit from the branches and bit into it, feeling the juice dribble down her chin.

What was this place? How did it exist? Here, in the deepest parts of the forest where the shadows should have been at their strongest, was a place where the darkness seemed to fade away.

She stayed there for three days, sleeping peacefully by night and wandering the clearing in a blissful trance by day. The rock pool never dried up. The tree never ran out of fruit.

But on the fourth day, she received a visitor.

The figure at the edge of the clearing resembled a man, but his features were cloaked in shadow. She could not see his face, but she knew he was watching her, and that he meant her harm.

She approached the stranger. She should have been afraid, but she felt safe within the clearing. Somehow, she knew he could not touch her in here.

She stopped a few feet away from him, and the two of them stood silently, watching each other.

Finally, she spoke.

"I'm not afraid of you."

The shadowy figure cocked its head to the side, amused.

"Because you think you are safe."

Each time it spoke, she thought she heard a thousand screams of agony, as though carried on the wind.

It continued, "You are not the first to seek sanctuary here. Many before you have tried. They all believed they were safe, but in time, I came for them."

The trees rustled. She felt another presence here. The shadowy features of the figure before her twisted in rage.

"No," she said, "that's a lie."

The stranger's head swivelled in a way that made her skin crawl. It seemed to be scanning the clearing for something, or someone. Then it returned its gaze to her.

"We shall see," it said, before retreating into the darkness of the forest.

She returned to the tree, lay down beneath it, and fell into a peaceful sleep.

The Watcher

Never think that you are safe from the one who watches.

Christof had learned this lesson well. He had seen all his friends taken by the beast, one by one. Whether or not they were dead, he couldn't say, but they had vanished without a trace.

Only a few were left. They called it the Watcher, for whenever it appeared, it said nothing and did nothing. It simply stood and silently beheld its victim. Its head was shaped like a jackal's, and its expression was cloaked in shadow.

And whenever it appeared, the target of its gaze disappeared, without even a scream or a cry for help.

The Watcher was not like the shadow creatures that dwelt deep within the forest. The shadow creatures left a corpse behind when they made a kill. The Watcher took its victims silently, and to who knew where?

It had first appeared months ago. Hendrik was the first to see it. No one believed him at the time. A few days later, Hendrik was gone.

Then others began disappearing. Christoff had seen the creature for himself when Jonah was taken. They'd been gathering berries by the river. Jonah was on the opposite bank. Christoff found a clump of berries and turned to call Jonah, but he had vanished.

In his place stood the Watcher. Christoff didn't hesitate. He turned and ran, and when he glanced back to see if the creature was following, he saw it standing in the exact spot it had appeared, shimmering like a reflection in the water.

In the beginning, they thought they would be safe so long as they remained within the encampment. Only people who ventured into the forest had been taken.

But then, one night, as they gathered around the campfire, they saw a shape in the darkness. The creature was standing on the outskirts of the camp.

Christoff grabbed a burning piece of wood and waved it at the creature. "What do you want!" he cried. "What do you want from us!" The others cowered in terror.

The Watcher said nothing and made no move towards them. Then it was gone.

The next day, another member of their group disappeared. The victim's hut was empty, and there were no signs of struggle.

Christoff's companions trembled with fear. They paced up and down the campsite. Some wanted to flee, others wanted to fight. If they fled then where would they go? Deeper into the forest, where they would be taken by the shadow creatures?

And how could they fight the creature when they didn't even know what it was?

Nonetheless, they resolved to resist in whatever way they could. They sharpened sticks to make spears. They piled stones around the campsite to form a barrier.

It didn't help. Maria woke up screaming during the night. They rushed to her aid and found her trembling at the entrance to her hut. "I saw it!" she cried. "Outside my window!"

They stayed with her to keep watch in case the creature returned.

The next morning, they realised Ricard was missing. They checked his hut. It was empty.

There were only three of them left now. Christoff, Larson and Maria. They decided to flee. They would probably die out there, but it was better than sitting around and waiting for The Watcher to take them.

They left the vine-encrusted huts that had been their haven for so long, and ventured into the forest, armed only with sharpened sticks.

Soon enough, they discovered to their dismay that the creature was not haunting the encampment, it was haunting them. It followed them into the forest.

They set up camp for the night, hoping they had made enough distance. They took turns to keep watch. Maria took the last watch, and when the other two woke up, she was gone.

There was nowhere to run, and no way to fight it. Christoff said they should go back to the encampment and await their fate. Larson wanted to go deeper into the forest.

They decided to part ways. Maybe if they split up, then one of them would escape.

Christoff returned to the camp and sat by the campfire. For days he had woken up in fear, gone to sleep in fear, never able to get the image of the Watcher out of his mind. But the fear was fading now. He would accept whatever came.

Peace came over him for the first time in months. Then he saw something in his mind's eye, the image of a man. The man was dressed in a cloth robe, and he sat on a stone altar in the middle of a cave.

The man looked up at him, smiled, and said, "Who watches the Watcher?"

Then he was gone.

Christoff waited for hours, pondering the strange dream. Finally, the Watcher arrived and stood at the edge of the firelight.

"What do you want from me? Why are you doing this?" Christoff asked.

For the first time, the Watcher spoke.

"What do you want from me. Why are you doing this?" it whispered, in a child-like voice.

"Where did you take the others?" said Christoff.

"Where did you take the others?" the Watcher responded.

Was the creature mocking him? It was hard to tell without seeing its face, but there was no malice in its voice.

The forest faded. Christoff felt like he was falling into the sky.

Then it was all black. Just him and the Watcher, surrounded by nothingness.

Christoff felt awareness begin to fade. He knew that if he fell asleep, he would be gone, like the others. He tried to fight it, but it was dragging him down like a weight around his legs.

Then he remembered what the man in his vision had said, and he decided not to fight it. He surrendered to the darkness. The Watcher was disappearing.

Suddenly, he felt something lift him. There was a light in the sky.

The Watcher cocked his head to the side, as if curious.

"You are not like the others," it said.

Christoff found himself responding in the only way that seemed appropriate.

"You are not like the others," he said.

The forest was coming back into view, the night sky was pierced by twinkling stars.

And there he was, back in front of the campfire. The warmth shielded him from the night.

The Watcher was still there. It gazed at him for a few moments, then it sat cross-legged on the other side of the campfire.

Christoff didn't move, didn't say anything.

He simply watched The Watcher.

The Tree God

In a part of the forest that few dare venture, the trees are gnarled and twisted, for they conceal a terrible presence.

Listen closely, and you can hear it. The sounds of weeping, screaming, and fists banging against wood.

The sounds are not coming from the trees. They are coming from within the trees.

Within each tree, someone is imprisoned. They struggle desperately, but cannot free themselves from their prison. They are completely encased in bark, unable to move a limb. Overcome with terror, they scream for help, but no one hears.

Two figures, a man and a woman, traipsed silently through the forest.

William glanced at Sarah, his wife of ten years, who had joined him on this deadly quest. He had tried to convince her to stay in the village, but she was determined to accompany him. Though he feared for her, he was moved by her courage.

Jerryn was his brother, taken by the one they called the Tree God two years ago, and William owed it to his brother to do what he could to free him. But Sarah had no such obligation. Only a bond of blood or love could convince one to undertake this deadly quest, and although

Sarah had always been fond of Jerryn, he was not her blood.

It was Sarah who had spoken to the wise woman and sought her counsel on how one could find the Tree God and convince him to release a prisoner. The wise woman assured her that the Tree God never killed his victims; he simply imprisoned them and fed off their life force.

An offering could be made to the Tree God, and if it was accepted, someone might be returned to the world of the living. But if the offer was rejected; well, the Tree God was not lenient with intruders.

But what could they offer the Tree God? Again, Sarah had found the answer. The wise woman told her where she could acquire a precious jewel, the likes of which had been coveted by the people who lived in this valley even before the cataclysm. She had ventured out alone and brought the jewel back with her, along with knowledge of how to find the Tree God.

Now there was nothing for it but to take this offering to the Tree God and hope for the best. William tried to convince Sarah that she had more than done her part, and should remain within the safety of the village. But she was determined to accompany him.

The ground grew soggy underfoot, a sign that they were approaching the Tree God's lair, which was said to be a fetid swamp where nothing grew. No one knew for certain what the Tree God was, only that it had existed as long as anyone in the village could remember and had perhaps been here even before the cataclysm.

They stopped to set up camp for the night. They could sleep safely in the open here, as the entities that haunted the forest stayed away from this place. Nonetheless, they took turns to keep watch. When Sarah's turn came, William lay down to rest. He woke up every now and then, and could hear Sarah sobbing and whispering to herself.

They awoke the next morning and continued their journey. After a few hours, the sounds of birds faded, replaced by the buzz of flies that gathered around the murky pools and rotting tree stumps.

Eventually, they arrived in a clearing, surrounded by a maze of trees with leafless branches reaching out in despair.

"This is the place," said William. There was a particularly large tree in the centre of the clearing, with a thick trunk and two knotholes that looked like eyes.

It was so quiet here, yet he was sure he could hear distant voices. They seemed to be coming from the trees surrounding the clearing.

Sarah watched as William slowly approached one of the trees. Yes, there was definitely a human voice, but where was it coming from?

He drew closer and pressed his ear against the tree trunk.

It was coming from within the tree! He could hear the muffled sound of someone sobbing, begging.

"There's someone in here!" He turned to Sarah, who was standing with her arms wrapped around herself.

"Sarah, did you hear me? There's…"

Suddenly, a shuddering sound came from the tree in the centre of the clearing. Its branches began to twist as though wracked with spasms of pain.

What he had at first thought to be a deformity in the tree trunk began to twitch and move, revealing itself to be a creature that had merged with the tree. It moved its head, then the rest of its body as it stepped out into the open; the bark of the tree clinging to it like wet mud.

The thing that now stood before them barely resembled a human, with coal-black eyes and a tangle of vines in place of arms. It towered over them, rising up to at least three times the height of a man, though its legs were bent like those of a praying mantis poised to strike.

William dropped to his knees and prostrated himself before the creature. Whether this being was god or monster was not for him to say, but the survival of any who confronted it depended on treating it with deference.

"Please…" he said, "Please, oh great one. I have come to beg for the life of another, one whom you hold prisoner in your kingdom."

These were the words he had been told to speak. He removed the jewel from the pocket of his breeches and laid it on the ground in front of him.

The Tree God looked at the jewel and laughed. It was a horrifying, guttural sound, like that of trees collapsing in the forest. William's heart sunk.

"You think this bauble can buy life?" it said. The trees around the clearing trembled as the creature spoke.

"The offering has already been made and accepted." Its eyes fell on Sarah, who was watching William with tears in her eyes.

William had rehearsed this moment so many times in his mind, but this turn of events had not come up in any of the scenarios he had envisioned. "No..." he said, as the meaning of the creature's words dawned on him. "No, please, not her..."

"Only life pays for life," the Tree God said.

"No... I refuse... " He rose to his feet.

"Sarah, run!" The creature turned back to him and laughed again. "Fear not, fool. It is not her life that was offered."

William looked at Sarah, then back at the Tree God. He didn't understand.

"Sarah, what does it mean? What..."

"I'm sorry, Wil," Sarah said, choking on her tears, "I'm so sorry."

The Tree God lifted one of its arms, and vines sprang from it towards William like a snake striking at prey. They entangled him and bound him to the spot.

Then, with its other arm, the monstrosity reached out towards one of the trees on the edge of the clearing. The vines dug into the bark, seized hold of something, and pulled it out. It was a man, taken out from within the very tree trunk.

Jerryn dropped to his knees, shuddering and gasping for breath as though he had just been pulled out of a freezing lake.

Sarah ran over to him and wrapped an arm around him, helping him to his feet. She embraced him, and the manner of the embrace told William all he needed to know. The nature of the situation finally dawned on him.

"Sarah!" cried William. "Sarah, please!" The Tree God turned towards him, its otherworldly gaze twisted in mockery.

Sarah didn't respond to his pleas. She wouldn't even look at him.

"The deal has been made," said the Tree God, "the price will be paid."

The vines that entangled William lifted him off the ground and carried him towards one of the trees. He clawed desperately at the ground, leaving finger marks in the soil.

The vines pinned him roughly against the tree, and he felt himself sinking slowly into the trunk as though it were quicksand. "No!" he cried in horror.

His cries were silenced as he disappeared into the tree trunk.

Jerryn was still gasping for breath, unaware of his surroundings. Sarah took his arm around her shoulder, and together they left the clearing. Behind them, the Tree God returned to his tree, merging with the trunk and disappearing from sight.

The Greatest Gift

Nikolai crashed through the underbrush as he ran, the forest looming around him. Just a few feet behind him, Ivan and Tomi followed. All three of them had run much further and faster than they would've thought themselves capable, but such is the power of fear.

Finally, they could run no more. They stopped and leaned over as they gasped for breath.

"We just have to outrun it," said Tomi.

Nikolai wasn't so sure. He wanted to keep going, but Tomi had clearly reached his limit. He leant against a tree, sliding down the trunk into a seated position. Ivan's eyes were darting from side to side as he scanned the forest.

Then Nikolai realised something that made his skin prickle. The forest had gone completely silent.

"We need to keep moving," he whispered as he went over to Tomi and hauled him to his feet. Tomi groaned and slid back down.

"I can't, I need a few more minutes," he said, "we must have outrun it by now."

"What if there's more than one?"

Tomi didn't respond. Nikolai scanned the forest for refuge. Ivan came to stand alongside him.

Suddenly, there was a piercing screech. Nikolai and Tomi spun around in alarm to see a shadow approaching through the distant trees.

"Get up!" he yelled at Tomi. He moved towards him, but Ivan was faster. He ran up to Tomi and pulled him to his feet.

Nikolai fought the urge to run. He wasn't going to leave his friends behind.

Suddenly, he heard a sickening snapping sound, and Tomi screamed out in pain. Nikolai turned to see him clutching his ankle. His attention had been so firmly fixed on the shadow that he had not seen what happened.

"What..."

The words caught in his throat as Ivan moved closer to Tomi, grabbed his head and smashed it against the tree. Tomi slunk to his knees, dazed.

"What are you doing!" yelled Nikolai as Ivan ran past him.

Tomi tried to take a few steps but fell down to his knees again, wincing in pain. "Help... help me," he said through a stream of tears.

Then the shadow was upon them. Nikolai watched in horror as it glided towards Tomi and wrapped itself around him like a cloak.

Tomi gave a blood-curdling scream as he was lifted a few feet into the air, arms outstretched. He started spinning around, crying out in agony.

His skin drained of colour. His limbs went into spasms. Nikolai could see his veins.

Then another shadow appeared in the distance.

Nikolai turned and ran.

He could see Ivan some distance ahead of him. Ivan would have to stop to catch his breath at some point and Nikolai would probably catch up to him; what would he do then? He wouldn't have called Ivan a close friend, but he had known him his whole life and would never have thought him capable of what he had just done.

Suddenly, Ivan disappeared. It looked like he had just sunk into the ground.

Nikolai reached the point and found that a hole had indeed opened and swallowed Ivan. It was some kind of pit trap. Who would have the courage to plant one this far out in the forest? Maybe it was there from a long time ago; it could have been over a hundred years old for all he knew.

Ivan was lying at the bottom of the pit, motionless. Nikolai glanced behind him; the shadows were nowhere to be seen, but it was only a matter of time before they caught up to him. His best chance for survival was to climb down into the pit and hide.

He reached the bottom and checked Ivan's pulse. He was dead. He must have broken his neck in the fall.

Now that Nikolai was inside the pit, he saw that it opened into an underground tunnel, dark and ominous, yet his only means of escape. Bracing himself, he entered.

The tunnel grew ever darker, and Nikolai, without any light source, struggled to maintain his footing. Every now and then something soft and sticky brushed up against him;

probably a spider-web. The image of Tomi floating in the air, screaming, as the shadow sucked the life out of him, burned in Nikolai's mind; suffocating what little hope he had left.

But then, after several hours of travelling the tunnel, he heard something strange. A sound unlike any he had heard before. It was some distance away, barely audible. Nikolai picked up the pace, drawn to the sound like a moth to flame.

Finally, he saw a glow in the distance, and a refreshing breeze touched his face. He carried on, coming upon the source of the light to see that it was indeed an exit from the tunnel; an opening to the surface, similar to the pit he had entered through. He clambered up eagerly, reinvigorated now that he could hear the distant sound more clearly.

The sunlight gently caressed his face as he made his way towards the sound, but he had gone no more than a few feet when he saw something that made him freeze in his tracks.

"No, it can't be," he whispered. There was a shadow hovering close by, although it appeared unaware of his presence. This was strange, as from what he had heard they could sense the presence of life.

He turned to run, but despair took him as he saw there was yet another shadow in his path, hovering silently like the other.

As he looked around, he could see the vague outline of the shadows everywhere. He was surrounded.

It seemed that he was meant to die this day. He resolved to try and reach the source of the sound he had heard in the tunnel before that happened. It was so beautiful to hear, that whatever was creating it must be beautiful to see. Perhaps he would get to see it before he died.

As he moved through the forest, he saw more shadows along his path, but they made no move towards him. In fact, they weren't moving at all, just hovering as though asleep.

The sound grew louder and louder, until finally the trees parted and he found himself in a clearing. There, in the centre, sitting on a stump, was a man with a strange object in his hand. It looked similar to a bow but larger and with more strings. As the man plucked at the strings, Nikolai realised that they were the source of the sound.

He stood watching for a while, letting the sound wash over him. He felt a lump in his throat as he listened.

Suddenly the man, whose attention had been fixed on the device in his hands, stopped and raised his head.

Disappointed that the sound had stopped, but realising the man was now aware of his presence, Nikolai stepped forward and greeted him. The man turned. He had long grey hair down to his shoulders, a clean-shaven face and pale eyes.

"A guest," he said, nodding and smiling. "I receive so few of them these days. What is your name, my friend?"

"Nikolai."

The old man noticed Nikolai staring at the instrument and held it up. "I assume you've never seen one of these before. It's called a harp."

"No, I've never seen one, but I could hear it from far away. It's the most beautiful sound I've ever heard."

"Why, thank you, young man."

Nikolai looked confused, not understanding why the old man was thanking him. The man seemed to guess what he was thinking.

"There is a skill to it, you know," he said, tilting his head forward and lowering his brow as if explaining something to a child, "and I've been playing for a long time... Not much else to do out here after all."

He began plucking at the strings of the harp again. It was a sad, haunting sound, but it soothed Nikolai and made him feel at peace. It spoke to something within him.

"Now tell me, how did you come to be all the way out here? As I said, it's been a long time since I've had visitors."

"I was looking for berries with two of my friends from the village. One of... the shadows attacked us. We ran."

"I gather your friends did not make it," said the man softly. Nikolai shook his head.

"I saw shadows on the way here. They were just floating in the air, doing nothing."

"Yes, the music seems to have that effect on them."

Music. So that's what the sound was called. Nikolai had heard the word before.

"Why?"

"Your guess is as good as mine. Music can be sad; music can be happy; but whatever type of music I play seems to hold them in place. For now, anyway."

The old man stopped playing and looked down at a patch of grass next to the stump. "This is not the only instrument I have, you know."

He rested the harp against the stump, and picked up an object that had been lying buried in the grass.

"This is my flute," he said. It looked like a small stick with holes in it. Nikolai couldn't picture such a device making any sound worth hearing, but when the old man lifted it to his mouth and began to play, the music was simple and sweet. It made him think of nights gathered around the fire in the middle of the village, drinking warm brew and talking with the others; the darkness of the surrounding valley melting away just for a short while

The man finished playing. "A much happier tune, isn't it?"

"Where did you find these…?"

"Instruments."

"Instruments. I need to find one for my village."

"They were passed down to me by my father, who received it from his father, and so on. They are gifts from the world that used to be. As to where you can find them, I fear you would have to travel some distance."

Nikolai's heart sunk. He could try bring some of the villagers here, but the journey would be dangerous, and there was no guarantee he'd find this place again.

"Why don't you come back with me? We could find a place for you in the village. You wouldn't even have to help with any of the daily tasks; you could just play your instruments."

"I appreciate the offer, but I prefer it out here. I find the solace comforting, and it helps with my music."

"The music might not work forever. You'd be safer with other people."

"Would I?"

Nikolai was about to respond, but then the image of Ivan smashing Tomi's head against the tree came into his mind.

The old man looked at Nikolai knowingly, then reached down to pick up the harp again. He resumed his sad tune.

Nikolai sat listening for a while, then reluctantly rose from the ground where he had been sitting.

"I must try to find my way back. I doubt we'll meet again." He turned to head back into the forest.

"Wait," said the old man, "I won't let you go back to your people empty-handed."

He picked up the flute in one hand, still holding the harp with the other, then laid them both on the ground in front of Nikolai. "Choose one."

Nikolai's eyes widened.

"You... you would give me one? Just like that?"

"Like I said, I have so few guests, nor any child to pass these onto. You could have taken these instruments by force; I cannot reward your good nature by watching as you march to your death."

His voice lowered as he said, "And die you will, if you go back in there alone."

Nikolai looked back and forth between the flute and harp.

"So, which will it be? Songs of sadness, or songs of good cheer?"

Finally, Nikolai reached for the harp.

"So you choose the one that weeps. I would've thought the flute more desirable."

"Well…" said Nikolai thoughtfully, "I feel like the harp knows me better."

"Indeed. It's good to have a friend who shares your sadness."

Nikolai plucked at the strings clumsily.

"I won't get far with that," he said.

"You'll get better. But stay a while, and I'll teach you a tune that will at least see you on your way home."

A couple of hours later, Nikolai felt ready to start his return journey, armed with the new tune. The cheerful sound of the man's flute followed him as he headed deeper into the forest.

Ghosts of the River

Sergei dipped his toes into the cool river water; a delightful shiver creeping up his spine.

They had been warned many times not to bathe in the river at night, but he didn't give any heed to the old folktales, and neither would the other villagers if they knew the pleasures it brought.

He took off his shirt and stepped deeper into the water, until it came up to his waist. It was icy cold; just what his body craved. Deeper he went until he was up to his shoulders. Then finally, he sank beneath the surface and stayed there a few seconds before reemerging.

He rubbed his eyes and ran his hands back through his long, shaggy brown hair. The river current pressed gently against him as he floated just a few feet from the shore. After what must have been an hour, he decided it was time to head back to the village, as reluctant as he was to do so.

As he was making his way towards the shore, he realised something that disturbed him. The sounds of river life that normally accompanied his bathing had ceased, and an ominous silence hung in the air.

He stopped, pondering this strange occurrence. The wise course of action was probably to make for the shore and return to the village as soon as possible, but it bothered him to have his normally serene bathing experience interrupted. He wanted to assure himself there was nothing to worry about so that he could return here next time without any lingering uncertainty.

He turned slowly, scanning the area for any sign of life.

Then, suddenly, a gravelly voice pierced the silence, uttering simply one word.

"Fool."

Sergei spun around, searching desperately for the source of the voice. "Who's there?" he cried.

"Fool. To bathe in my waters, to laugh in the face of the night."

Sergei saw a ripple in the surface, then watched in horror as a shape slowly emerged from the water. First came webbed hands with claws, then two eyes glaring at him with hatred. As it rose further from the depths, he saw before him a large, frog-like creature, water spilling down its slimy skin. It was the size of at least four horses put together.

Sergei turned and fled for the shore of the river, but the water had altered its flow and was now pulling him back towards the creature. He struggled desperately against the current.

The creature laughed; a sound like two boulders crashing together.

"Please, let me go!"

The creature drew closer and reached out with one of its webbed hands, wrapping it around Sergei and binding him tightly.

"No, I will not do that. You will die now, human, and serve me in death."

Sergei screamed for help, but there was no one to hear him. The creature laughed in response to his screams, and sank beneath the surface, dragging him with it.

The screams stopped abruptly as he disappeared beneath the surface, and the shores of the river were quiet once again.

***

Jaro dipped his hand in the river and splashed some water over his face. His boat drifted gently along the surface, and he thanked the heavens that he had not yet encountered any rapids. He did not want to have to drag the boat overland.

He had been fortunate to find the boat, abandoned yet in perfect working order. He wondered who it had belonged to before, and how long it had lain there beneath the weeds.

Here, on the river, he felt safe from whatever roamed the forest. Of course, he had to return to the shore occasionally to forage for food, but at least he knew he could flee back to the boat if he encountered any danger. Unless someone stole the boat while he was away, but that was unlikely. It had been some time since he had glimpsed any sign of human life.

That would change today however, for as he guided the boat along a bend in the river, he glimpsed a figure in the distance. It seemed to be moving back and forth along the shore.

As he drew closer, he saw that it was a man, holding a pitchfork. He appeared to be tilling the soil on the shores of the river.

Jaro was baffled by the sight. He had not seen encountered any human life for months; let alone a man engaging in such a pointless task. What on earth was he doing?

He closed the distance, and the man's features became clearer. He was bare-chested, with long, shaggy brown hair falling down to his broad shoulders.

Jaro called out to him, and the man looked up, but his expression sent a shiver down Jaro's spine. His gaze was empty, and his eyes devoid of life. Jaro may as well have been looking at the face of a corpse.

The man didn't respond. He watched Jaro in silence for a few moments, then turned his attention back to his aimless task.

Jaro grabbed an oar and began rowing, hoping to get away from the man as fast as possible. He was relieved when the figure disappeared.

It was getting dark and Jaro was considering anchoring the boat and preparing for night, when he saw the surface of the water ripple. He watched in shock as a human hand emerged from the water, followed by a head, then the torso of a man as he clawed his way onto the shore. He too was carrying a pitchfork, and as he stood up, he began to till the soil on the shore of the river just as the previous man had done.

Jaro lay down in the boat, attempting to hide from this apparition. He remained there as the boat continued to float down the river. It grew darker, until he couldn't see but could only hear a splash every now and then and the sound of another being climbing onto the shore.

He was sailing along a river of ghosts.

Too afraid to anchor the boat, he fell asleep while cowering within it. He awoke at first light to find that the boat had stopped. He dared to sit up and look. The vessel had crashed into an old water mill, which was barring its passage down the river.

Glad to have encountered some form of human civilisation, he pulled the boat onto the shore and went to investigate the mill. It was in a sorry state, and it was clear that it had been abandoned for some time.

Suddenly, he heard a gravelly voice behind him.

"Fool. To wander my river."

He turned to see a strange creature emerging. Water dripped from its frog-like head as it rose, and its hateful eyes were fixed on him. It began moving towards him; its twisted torso and monstrous size revealed as it approached the shore.

Jaro turned and ran for the cover of the mill, hearing a ferocious snap behind him as the creature cleaved his boat in two.

He stumbled into the mill, slamming the door shut behind him, and hid amongst the machinery. The creature, too large to fit through the doorway, began to hammer the wall with webbed hands.

"Once I have taken you, I will crush this pathetic structure," it said, "for I despise humanity and all its works."

Timbers shattered and split apart as the creature's fist plunged through the wall, creating a hole just big enough for one slitted eye to peer inside. It rolled around in its socket as the creature scanned the interior, and eventually fell on the wheel Jaro was hiding behind. Then it resumed its assault, the hole growing larger as splinters of wood sprayed out, some of them hitting Jaro as he cowered against the opposite wall.

Realising the creature was moments away from penetrating the mill, Jaro crawled out through a window and was about to flee into the forest when he glimpsed a figure approaching through the trees. It seemed to be hovering in the air, and there was surely only one thing it could be.

He was trapped.

Then the creature burst through the wall of the mill; splinters flying in every direction. Jaro ducked and threw his arm up in front of his face, and those few moments cost him. He felt an iron grip close around his leg as the creature seized him. He fell over and clawed at the ground desperately as the monster dragged him towards the river.

The water was freezing cold; colder than he remembered it being. As he was dragged into the river, he reached out desperately for something; anything to grab hold of. But it was hopeless. The water came up to his waist, then his chest, then his neck. He gave one last desperate cry as his head was swallowed by the muddy shallows.

Suddenly, something grabbed his wrist and began to pull. He coughed out water as his head popped above the surface, and he saw someone standing over him. It looked like a man, but he was surrounded by light that concealed his features.

The creature emerged to see what had taken hold of its prey. "You!" it snarled. Such was its shock at seeing the man that it released Jaro from its grip, allowing his saviour to pull him out of the river.

Jaro stumbled onto the shore, dripping wet and trembling. The stranger turned his attention to the beast.

"You've claimed enough souls, Vodyanoy."

"You don't have the power to stop me."

"I do now."

The stranger reached out towards the beast, holding up his hand like a shield. Suddenly light burst forth from the creature's eyes, then its mouth. Its limbs froze, and its gravelly voice shook the forest as it cried out.

Slowly, it sunk beneath the surface of the river.

The stranger helped Jaro to his feet.

"Who are you?" Jaro asked in awe. Through the glow that surrounded the man, he could barely make out a face, with eyes that were white and rippling like the surface of a tranquil pool.

"I cannot stay here any longer," the man said, "it's taken most of my strength to appear in this form. I'm afraid your question will have to go unanswered. Perhaps one day, we'll meet again."

He pointed in the direction that the river flowed. "The river is safe for now. Follow it for three days and you will find a village."

With that, the man's form slowly faded, and Jaro was alone. Alone, but alive.

He followed the river as the stranger had suggested and saw no more ghosts upon the shore.

The Man Beast

"What could have done this?" Liara looked around the village in horror. Bodies were strewn across the ground, blood marks on the walls of the huts. The population had been exterminated.

"Not what. Who," said Tavik as he appeared alongside his younger companion. He pointed at the bodies. "These wounds were made by weapons. Humans did this."

He was right. The violence was so savage as to seem the work of beasts, but the evidence showed that it was men, not creatures of the forest.

Jerryn emerged from behind them; his footsteps crunching on the ground. He had been investigating the huts.

"No survivors," he said. "It doesn't look like a raid either; most of the huts are still stocked with supplies. This was pure murder."

Liara shivered. Men, women and children ruthlessly butchered.

"Let's gather what we can and be on our way," said Tavik.

As callous as it felt sifting through the people's possessions, they grabbed what provisions they could find before moving on, glad to leave the village behind them.

They'd been travelling for some time when Tavik raised his hand. "Halt," he said. As the oldest member of the group, Liara and Jerryn had come to respect his authority. They also relied on the sixth sense he seemed to have when navigating the forest.

"Tracks," he said, pointing at the ground. Liara wouldn't have noticed anything without Tavik's direction, but following his lead, she was able to make out some trampled underbrush.

"They could be the ones that wiped out the village," said Jerryn. "We should move on."

"Could be," said Tavik. His eyes flicked from side to side as he scanned the environment.

Jerryn sighed. Liara knew what he was thinking. Tavik wouldn't be able to resist the urge to explore further.

"Stay here, I'll have a look around. We need to know what we're dealing with."

He vanished into the forest and returned an hour later.

"There's a cave. Could be a good place to spend the night."

"Any tracks?"

"Not that I could see."

Darkness was descending. Liara liked the idea of having shelter for once, but Jerryn was reluctant.

"Did you check inside the cave?"

"It's a cave. How many people could there be? Certainly not enough to wipe out a village."

Jerryn shook his head. "I don't like it. We need to get far away from this area."

"We've been sleeping out in the open for weeks," said Liara, "how long before we get another opportunity like this? I say we take our chances."

Tavik looked Jerryn and raised an eyebrow questioningly.

"Fine," said Jerryn, "but we search the cave thoroughly first."

Tavik led them to the spot. They weren't prepared for what they found inside.

"'How many could there be', you said," muttered Jerryn, "this place could hold at least a hundred people."

At the back of the cave was a tunnel that looked man-made. Further down, they could see it crisscross with other tunnels, forming a network of passageways.

"There's at least one person here already," said Liara, pointing to the side of the cave where there was a pot, a skinning rack and a fur mattress.

"We should leave immediately," said Jerryn but Tavik didn't seem to hear him. He was busy inspecting the other side of the cave, where the wall was adorned by paintings. There were depictions of deer and other animals in the forest. Curiously, one of the paintings showed two men and a wolf, walking in single file.

Liara approached the wall and traced a finger along the drawings. "They're beautiful."

"Beautiful, and ancient," said a voice behind them.

They turned sharply to see a man standing at the entrance to the cave. He was carrying a pile of firewood.

As he stepped into the cave, Liara saw that he was dressed in furs, and had a grizzled face. He seemed intensely alert; not fearful and half-mad like the other loners they had met in the forest.

"Whoever crafted them was here long before us."

Liara could feel the tension emanating from Tavik and Jerryn. Fearing they would go for their weapons, she tried to pre-empt any potential hostility.

"We're sorry for intruding," she said, "we were looking for a safe place to spend the night. We've been wandering the forest for weeks." She decided not to mention the massacre they had seen earlier in the day.

The man shrugged. "The cave doesn't belong to me."

He carried the firewood to the side of the cave and dumped it next to the pot.

"My name is Casmir," he said as he dusted his hands off. "You're welcome to stay here."

"I'm Liara, and this is Tavik and Jerryn," said Liara. Her two companions relaxed slightly.

"You don't get any trouble out here?" asked Tavik.

"I've been lucky so far." Casmir picked up some logs of wood and carried them to the centre of the cave, where he sat down and lit a fire.

Liara couldn't resist the warmth. She moved forward and crouched down beside the fire, holding her hands up to the flame. Tavik and Jerryn exchanged looks, then warily approached the fire and did the same.

"There is… was a village nearby," said Jerryn.

Casmir said nothing.

"All the people are dead," Tavik finished Jerryn's question for him. "What happened?"

"Slaughtered… by men," Casmir emphasised the 'by men' part, "but you need not fear the ones who did it. They have no quarrel with you."

"You're saying it was some kind of feud?"

Casmir nodded. "Something like that."

They sat in silence as it grew dark outside. After a time, Casmir rose and went to the cave entrance.

"I have to go," he said, before vanishing into the night.

The three companions were unsure what to make of that. They decided to set up a watch. The fire and the protection of the cave provided comfort, but they didn't know anything about their host.

Liara's turn to keep watch came last, just as the sun was rising. It was then that Casmir returned, with a deer slung over his back.

"You were hunting?" asked Liara suspiciously. Casmir didn't respond. He laid the deer on the skinning rack at the side of the cave and went to lie on the fur mattress.

A few days passed. Casmir continued to hunt during the night and sleep during the day. The three companions were discomfited by this but were reluctant to leave the safety of the cave. So, they remained, and over time, grew familiar enough with their host to sleep without posting a watch.

One day, whilst Casmir was out collecting firewood, three rugged men appeared at the cave entrance. Jerryn and Tavik took a few steps back, hands resting on the knives at their sides.

The man at the front ignored them as he scanned the cave. Eventually, he turned his attention to the cave's occupants.

"Where is Casmir?"

"Is he a friend of yours?" asked Tavik.

"He was once, but I doubt he would welcome us now. Thankfully, he's not here." The man gave an ugly smile. His tone put Liara on edge.

"We heard he had new friends," he continued, "you're brave to trust one such as him."

"He's not given us any reason to distrust him," answered Tavik.

"Don't you wonder about his hunting habits?"

Tavik had no reply. The man approached the paintings on the cave wall and traced a finger along the picture of the wolves.

"You know something about him we don't?" asked Jerryn.

The man ignored him. "Tell me, what do you see in this painting?"

"Two men and a wolf?"

"Really? I see a man, then a wolf, then a man."

Tavik and Jerry looked confused. The visitor continued, "And the two men look the same. Perhaps it's the same man?"

"Cavemen weren't known for their attention to detail," said Tavik.

The man laughed. "If you say so."

He turned to his two companions. "We've seen what we need to see. Let's avoid any awkward reunions."

He headed for the cave entrance. As he was about to leave, he turned and gave that same sinister smile.

"Ask Casmir what he makes of the painting. I'm sure he'll have much to say."

With that, he and his companions vanished into the forest.

When Casmir returned, he stopped at the cave entrance and sniffed the air.

"We've had visitors."

"Who were they?" asked Liara.

Casmir carried the firewood to the edge of the cave and dumped it in the usual spot.

"Old friends of mine. Probably came to see if I was sheltering survivors."

"Survivors? You mean from the village?"

"Yes. The slaughter was their work. Well, them and others."

He sat down beside them in the centre of the cave and lit a fire.

Tavik looked thoughtful. He was tracing patterns in the sand with a stick. "There are stories," he said, "of men who become wolves by night."

Jerryn looked up at Tavik, then at Casmir in alarm. His hand went to his knife.

Liara's eyes darted to the painting of the wolf and the two men. The stranger had been right; it was one man. Her hair prickled as she finally understood.

"It's said they've been in this valley a long time, long before the world collapsed."

Tavik looked up at Casmir. "'I'd want to know if I was in the presence of such a beast."

"A beast, you say?"

"An entire village was massacred."

"By men."

Casmir gazed into the fire. Tavik watched him for a few moments, then continued, speaking carefully, "You've been good to us, and we're grateful. But you can't blame us for being afraid. We've heard the stories."

Casmir finally looked up, firelight reflecting off his face.

"You're right. You deserve to know the truth. As it happens, I have a story for you as well."

***

Thousands of years ago, when man was still young, a band of hunters made their home in a network of caves carved out by ancients.

These were no normal hunters. By day, they lived as men, but by night, they became wolf-men, roaming the forest and hunting in the darkness. Where their strange power came from was lost in the mists of time.

But their clan grew at a slow pace, much slower than other clans that lived in the valley. As the nearby clans multiplied in numbers, they clashed with the wolf-men.

The wolf-men had the advantage at night, but during the day their enemies attacked with weapons. The wolf-men were limited by their beastlike nature, and thus unable to forge such weapons.

Much blood was spilt. Finally, after decades of fighting, a pact was made between the two clans. The wolf-men swore that they would only hunt animals, never men. In return, the human clan swore they would leave the wolf-men in peace.

The two clans met once a century in a sacred ceremony to renew their pact, and the peace lasted for over a thousand years.

But things changed when darkness fell on the world. The survivors who lived in the valley grew desperate. A nearby human clan now sought to expand their territory and seize additional resources. They launched one assault after another on the wolf-men's caves, fighting with fervour and more sophisticated weaponry. Despite their attempts to fight back, the wolf-men were reduced greatly in numbers, until they were on the verge of extinction.

It was then that they were approached by a stranger whose face was cloaked in shadows. He offered them a deal; he would remove the power that trapped them in the form of wolves at night. This would free them to develop human weapons and tactics to use against their enemies, instead of having to fight as animals.

In return, they would have to pledge themselves to him; build a shrine dedicated to him and sacrifice one of their own every five years to keep the power that made them wolf-men at bay.

All but one of the wolf-men agreed to this bargain. The one that rejected it sensed anger and bloodlust in his fellow wolf-men, and feared that this stranger, who he distrusted, would bring out the worst in them. He remained in the cave, while the others, no longer limited by their beast forms, left to found a new settlement.

They were consumed with the desire for vengeance against the enemy that had tormented them for so long. They set their minds on forging weapons and tools and came up with a plan to infiltrate the village.

Some of them posed as refugees seeking safety and were taken in by the humans, who had grown complacent since finding the wolf cave abandoned. The former wolf-men decided when they would enact their vengeance. On that night, the ones who had infiltrated the village rose up and attacked from within, while the others attacked from the forest.

It was a slaughter. The former wolf-men, driven by rage and bloodlust, killed every man, woman and child. Once their bloody work was done, they retreated into the forest.

***

Casmir's eyes had been fixed on the fire as he told his tale, which was followed by a long silence.

Tavik was the first to speak. "A sad story," he said, "how much is known about the stranger your... former friends made their bargain with?"

Casmir simply shook his head. He remained silent as they ate, but after he left to hunt, the three companions discussed their next course of action.

Jerryn insisted they could not remain. Tavik was inclined to agree.

"He may not be as savage as the rest of his kind, but he remains a half-beast. How long before his animal impulses overcome him?"

"I've not felt any danger since we've been here; I've felt safer than I have for years," argued Liara.

But Tavik and Jerryn were set on leaving, and Liara didn't like the idea of being alone with the wolf-man, as much as she had come to like him. So, the next day, they packed their things. Jerryn wanted to leave immediately, but Liara and Tavik agreed they should wait for their host to return so they could thank him. They owed him that at least.

Casmir returned with three rabbits attacked to his belt, took one look at the three of them with their possessions slung over their shoulders and went to hang his kills on the skinning rack. "I wish you well on your journey," he said.

As they left the cave and headed into the forest, Liara felt a familiar fear grip her; the fear that they would not make it to the next day. For there was much worse than beasts out here, in the darkness of the valley.

The Temple of Secrets

In the ruins of a monastery, a robed monk wandered the surrounding gardens, alone.

The days were hard for Stefan. They were long and devoid of colour. It was a struggle to keep himself occupied; to keep his mind from descending into the fog.

But at night, the monastery came alive, and he felt energy course through him. The torches that lined the halls ignited of their own accord, and strange spirits wandered the corridors. He didn't know where these silent ghosts came from, but they seemed to mean no harm.

At night, there was a refreshing chill in the air, and the gardens were illuminated by starlight, which reflected on the surface of the gentle stream that circled the monastery.

The forest loomed ominously in the distance, but he felt safe within the confines of the monastery, which had yet to be invaded by any of the sinister denizens of the valley.

In the centre of the monastery was a scriptorium, seemingly untouched despite the ruined state of its surroundings, and in the scriptorium was a book. Stefan came here in the evenings to record his dreams in the book. He craved knowledge of the mysteries of the valley, and recording his dreams in the book allowed him to relive the visions he experienced at night.

On one night, when his work was done, he closed the heavy, leather bound book and retired to his quarters. It was one of the few rooms in the monastery that remained mostly intact. There was a hole in the stone roof, and a section of the wall was crumbling, but he didn't mind. It provided a view of the star-studded sky, although sometimes it was pierced by cold winds.

He lay down on his straw mattress, wondering if any visions would be revealed to him during his slumber.

A dream did indeed come to him, although he would regret seeing what this dream had to show him.

He found himself floating above a mountain. It was part of the range that surrounded the valley but was taller than its neighbours. What truly set it apart was the nightmarish landscape that surrounded it.

The slopes of the mountain were bare, as though decimated by fire. There was no semblance of life for miles around, just blackened wasteland and dead trees.

Stefan floated towards the mountain. He wanted to leave this place, but some force was dragging him down. He approached the crumbling slopes, and as he drew closer, he saw the entrance to a cave, barely visible amidst the cloister of rocks.

The cave filled him with dread, but still, his journey continued. He passed through the entrance and into a tunnel that snaked its way deep into the mountain.

Eventually, he entered a large cavern with a circular stone platform in the centre.

A figure sat cross-legged upon the platform, and as Stefan drew closer, he saw that it was man clad in patched robes. He was skeletal, as though starved, and his jaw was tight.

Suddenly his eyes snapped open, and the look in them terrified Stefan, causing his incorporeal form to tremble like candlelight on the verge of being snuffed out by the wind.

The man's eyes contained hate that burned like fire. They turned to look sidelong at Stefan, then the man turned his whole head. Now all his attention was on his unwilling guest.

He snarled in rage, eyes blazing. The sound of thousands of voices crying in agony could be heard in the wind.

Stefan knew that if he remained here much longer, his consciousness would be destroyed by the chaotic power that emanated from the man's hateful gaze. Thankfully, whatever force had brought him here now pulled him back, through the tunnel and out the cave entrance, up into the sky.

He awoke, shivering. A cold wind was blowing through the crumbling walls of the chamber. There would be no sleep for him tonight, so he rose and paced the halls of the monastery. Spirits hovered silently around him as his mind raced. Who was the stranger, and what was the purpose of this vision?

The experience still haunted him the following day, and as evening came and he sat down before the Great Book, his hand trembled as he clutched the quill and began to write.

But as he was writing, with half a page complete, the words suddenly vanished, leaving the parchment blank.

He stared at the page in shock. After taking a few moments to collect himself, he made another attempt to record the dream. This time, the words vanished after only a few sentences.

He made several more attempts, but each time, the words vanished. On his final attempt, the words ceased to appear at all, even as his quill pressed against the page.

He looked up. A sense of dread descended on him, a feeling that there was some dark presence nearby.

Something had found the monastery, and it was aware of him.

He rose and made his way to the monastery entrance. There he stood, peering into the darkness of the night. He could barely make out the edge of the forest in the distance.

Something was watching him from behind the wall of trees. He shivered and went back to the halls of the monastery.

He returned to his quarters, where he crouched by the wall, looking up through the opening in the roof. The vastness of the starlit sky comforted him.

The next morning, he risked another look out the monastery entrance. This proved to be a mistake. In the light of day, he finally saw the source of the dread he had felt the night before. There were shadowy figures at the edge of the forest, watching the monastery.

He withdrew, trembling uncontrollably. Surely the creatures would have invaded the monastery by now if they could? He wondered if they could cross the river.

Even his quarters no longer felt safe. He decided to barricade himself in the scriptorium.

Night came and went. A cold wind battered the stone walls. Stefan was growing hungry but was afraid to go to the vegetable garden. He didn't know how long it would be before the creatures gained access to the monastery grounds. Perhaps he would die of starvation before they arrived?

After a night in the scriptorium, he couldn't bear it anymore. He went back to the entrance and saw that the shadows had drawn closer; they were now about a hundred feet from the river.

The next day, they were even closer, hovering on the riverbank. "What do you want?" Stefan cried out, but he was met with silence. The shadows were motionless.

That night, Stefan wandered the halls of the monastery. His fear gave way to resignation. Ghostly figures hovered around him, seemingly unperturbed by the creatures outside.

With nothing else to do, he returned to the scriptorium. Perhaps whatever force had prevented him from writing in the Great Book was gone. Then he could at least keep his mind occupied by recording what would probably be his last few days.

He opened the book and turned to the first blank page. expecting the words to vanish as he wrote. But to his surprise, he saw words start to appear on the page, as though written by an invisible hand.

As the words formed, he realised it was a series of directions, leading to a particular hallway in the monastery. He had passed through this hallway many times without thinking anything of it.

Then, as if in response to his confusion, a drawing began to form below the writing. It formed a circular shape with two short lines running diagonally across the centre.

He stared in amazement. For a moment, he forgot about the dark presence outside the monastery.

Then he rose and followed the directions laid out in the Great Book. He arrived in the marked corridor. At least half a dozen spirits were swirling around him.

So he had followed the directions, but what was he supposed to do next? As he stood in thought, a ghost suddenly emerged from the wall and floated away. He had never seen one of them pass through the wall like that.

He examined that portion of the wall. Like the rest of the monastery, it was made of stones covered in cracks and crevices.

Then he gasped. It was barely visible, but the cracks on one of the stones formed an image that matched that from the book; a rectangle with two lines scrawled diagonally across the centre.

Seized by an impulse, he pressed down on it.

There was a creaking sound as a door opened on the floor of the corridor. A cloud of dust spewed out and engulfed Stefan, causing him to cough violently.

He peered into the opening and saw a ladder. Clambering down it, he saw a tunnel passing under the wall, running straight ahead with no end in sight.

Gathering his courage, he started down the tunnel and disappeared into the darkness

The Bark-Skinned Man

It was late in the day when Clara first encountered the bark-skinned man.

She had wandered deeper into the forest than usual, and now she was drawn by the sound of the river. Her mother would be furious if she knew where she was, but Clara had longed to wander ever since she learned to walk.

She had grown especially curious about what lay outside the village over the past year, and each time she ventured into the forest, risked going a little further than she had the time before. On her fifth trip, she went far enough to reach the shore of the river. She was captivated by its beauty and power, and just the sound of it made her feel alive.

She decided to walk along the river bank to see where it would lead her.

She'd been walking for some time, and with sunset just a few hours away, she felt it was time to return to the village. But then she saw something that made her stop in her tracks. There was a figure of a man in the distance, sitting by the river with his back resting against a tree.

She never expected to encounter a human presence this far from the village. The man also had a strange posture. Long, thin legs like sticks, with a hunched upper body. He resembled a mantis.

The man turned to look in her direction, causing her to jump in surprise. She fled into the cover of the trees, running until she was out of breath. Eventually, she turned to see if anyone was following her, but there was nothing besides the gentle rustle of the trees.

It would be a long time before she entered the forest again. Her mother had grown ill, and Clara spent most of her time tending to her. The village healer visited every now and then to sprinkle some powders and perform some strange chants, but the only thing that helped was a broth she prepared to relieve the pain.

One day, Clara found herself wandering deep into the forest again, lost in sadness. She reached the river and walked along the bank. This time, she found herself hoping she would see the strange man.

And so she did. Her fear had given way to curiosity, and she decided to get a closer look. She approached carefully, using the forest as cover, until she was beside a tree just a few feet away from the man.

She peered from behind the tree and saw that the man's appearance was even stranger than what she had seen from afar. He had a long grey beard that fell down to his knees, and spindly fingers that resembled twigs. But strangest of all was his skin, which was like the bark of a tree. From head to toe, he was covered in bark.

She realised now what she was looking at. There were stories told in the village of a bark-skinned man who lived in the forest. Many dismissed them as folktales, yet here she was, staring at a folktale come to life.

Suddenly, the bark-skinned man spoke.

"You are far from home, child."

Clara was too taken aback to respond.

"What brings you out here?" He turned to look at her. His eyes were pure white and slightly creased at the sides, as though touched by sadness.

"Come to escape your troubles, perhaps?"

Clara's eyes welled up with tears. A sadness came over her that took her completely by surprise; the weight of the strain she had been struggling with for months bearing down on her.

She began to cry.

The trees rustled in response to her pain, and a cold breeze touched her face.

"You fear for someone you love?" The man's voice was gentle and kind.

Clara nodded.

"A father? A mother?"

"My mother. She's sick."

The bark-skinned man returned his gaze to the river.

"I see your pain, but also your courage. Whatever comes, you will have the strength to face."

Clara felt a burden lifted from her shoulders. She went to sit beneath a tree in line with the one against which the man was resting. The two of them watched the river in silence for a time.

Then, realising that darkness was a few hours away, Clara stood up.

"I have to go home now."

The bark-skinned man nodded. "I will be here, when you wish to speak of your troubles again."

Clara would return to that place again, many times. Sometimes, she would tell the bark-skinned man her fears, her hopes and her dreams. Other times, they would sit in silence and listen to the sounds of the river.

One day, she came to the bark-skinned man with tears streaming down her face.

"She's gone," she said. "My mother... she..."

She left the rest unspoken, and sat down by the tree, holding her knees to her chest. She sobbed quietly.

The bark-skinned man was silent for a time, and when he finally did speak, his voice was like the rustle of wind in the trees.

"Not gone," he said, "simply passed into another realm. But why do you hold back your tears, child? Let them flow like the river as it carries away the sand."

And Clara did cry, letting all the pain and fear pour out.

"You say she's gone to another place," she said, as she began to calm down, "but what if she's trapped here? They say there are whispers in the forest; people who have died, trapped here forever."

"No," said the bark-skinned man, "the whispers are the ghosts of pain, but no darkness can trap the soul."

Clara continued to visit the bark-skinned man as the days and weeks went on. He understood her pain in a way the other villages did not, and showed insight they were unwilling or unable to provide.

One day, she finally worked up the courage to ask the question she'd been meaning to ask for some time.

"All this time, I've never asked who you are, or where you came from."

The bark-skinned man was silent, a distant look in his eyes as he gazed at the river.

"I had a name once, but it was long ago. Now, I am what you see before you."

"But you must have come from somewhere. You can't have been sitting by this river all this time."

The bark-skinned man sighed. "Are you certain you wish to know the truth? It may be hard for one as young as you to understand." He turned to look at Clara.

Seeing the sadness in his eyes made her hesitate for a moment, but then she nodded. "Tell me."

***

Many centuries ago, when humanity still inhabited this land in great numbers, the nearby village was but one of many that dotted the countryside. But even still, the villagers kept to themselves and were suspicious of outsiders.

There was a man who lived apart from the rest of the village. He stayed in a hut in the forest, and since he had skill with herbs, villagers would sometimes visit him for remedies.

Some of the villagers muttered about witchcraft, but for the most part, they left him alone.

But that changed when the children began to disappear.

When the first child went missing, the village sent search parties into the forest, but found no trace of him. Then a second went missing, and panic seized the villagers.

A third went missing, then a fourth. The villagers, overcome with fear and dismay, searched for someone to blame. Suspicion immediately fell on the old hermit. He was an outsider, a loner, and whoever was responsible could not possibly be one of their own.

A bloodthirsty mob marched on the hermit's hut, and in their madness, dragged him into the forest and hung him from a tree by the river.

The trouble stopped for a short time, leading the villagers to think they had disposed of the culprit. But then children started disappearing once again. The one responsible had merely been lying low.

Then something miraculous happened. One of the children escaped, and revealed the identity of his kidnapper, who turned out to be one of the village's wealthiest and most respected inhabitants.

After the murderer was dealt with, some of the villagers regretted what they had done to the hermit. They went to the river to recover his body, so he could at least be given a proper burial. But the body had vanished.

***

Clara gazed at the bark-skinned man as he finished his tale. "That's... so unfair." It was the only word she could think of.

"Perhaps," said the bark-skinned man, "but sometimes good can come from bad. The hermit's spirit lived on, and where in life he had been accused of harming children, in death he became their protector. Now, no child need fear the darkness so long as he watches over the village."

He turned to look at Clara, his eyes like tranquil pools.

Clara returned to the village. As she walked through the forest, little did she know that just a short distance away, shadows lurked amidst the trees. They sensed the presence of life nearby and longed to descend on her and feed. But some power kept them at bay.

So they drifted on the outskirts, just beyond the reach of this power. They were ever-hungry, but hungry they would remain, so long as the bark-skinned man kept watch.

The Blackest Pit

It was Karl's time to enter the pit.

Who survived and who died in the pit, was a secret closely guarded. The reward for surviving was also unknown.

All the people of the tribe knew was that pit was dark and deep, but that the treasure contained within was more valuable than any that could be obtained.

But to retrieve it, you had to venture to the very bottom of the pit.

There were dangers along the way. There were nightmares and dead things and the remains of those who had gone before and failed.

Karl had reached his sixteenth year, and when you reached your sixteenth year, you were offered the choice. Enter the pit to try and retrieve the reward, risking death; or remain with the tribe. The latter offered safety and security, normalcy. A role would be found for you. The tribe needed people to gather food, keep watch, and take care of the children.

But if you entered the pit, and retrieved the treasure, it would grant you freedom. So it was said.

Freedom from what? Freedom to venture out into the world beyond and face whatever dangers lurked there. For the prize was powerful and granted protection against the demons of the forest.

Karl decided long ago he would choose the pit. He didn't know what role he could play within the tribe. He didn't feel suited to any of the tasks. The tribe would be better off without him.

This was his one chance to prove to himself that there was a reason for his existence.

There was only one other person with him here: Grenn, the oldest member of the tribe. It was said that the old man had survived the pit and spent time travelling the forest before returning. It was Grenn who guided people to the pit, and waited to see if they returned. He alone knew how many survived the ordeal.

Grenn was reclusive; he lived in a hut on the edge of the forest and rarely ventured into the village, and the children of the tribe were afraid to approach him. Karl remembered being afraid too, until the day he saw a different side of Grenn.

It was Grenn who had found him, alone in the forest, on the day he almost gave into the dark thoughts. There were times when a cloud descended on him, and he considered walking into the forest alone. To do so was certain death, but that was what he craved when the darkness came upon him.

The cloud was thick and heavy on that day, and he was on the verge of disappearing into the forest when he heard the old man's voice behind him:

"Your day to face the darkness will come. But it does not have to be today."

Grenn had sat and talked with him awhile, then brought him back to the village and gave him a broth to calm him down. Karl didn't have dark thoughts for a long time after that. He never had a chance to speak to Grenn since then, but he no longer feared him as the other children did.

And now, Grenn was with him on the day he would finally face the darkness.

The old man gazed at him silently. His face, surprisingly smooth for one his age, gave nothing away; not sympathy, regret, nor fear for Karl's safety. Whether or not he expected Karl to survive this trial, of that, his eyes betrayed no sign. He motioned towards the rope dangling from the edge of the pit.

"Your journey begins there," he said, "but at a certain point, you will run out of rope, yet still have some distance to go. All you will have left to hold onto will be your own resolve."

Karl nodded and grabbed onto the edge of the rope. He slid slowly into the pit.

"Good luck," Grenn said softly.

Karl had been climbing for some time, and his arms were starting to ache. The last glimmer of sunlight had long been swallowed by the dark.

He came past a skeleton embedded in the rock; its skull turned upward and its fingers clawing desperately against the walls of the pit. Whoever it once belonged to had been climbing up, not down. Perhaps the poor soul had given up the descent and attempted to retreat, only to find that the pit would not allow it.

Karl shuddered and continued his descent. He could hear whispers now, coming from somewhere below him. He felt a force pulling at his legs as if the pit were trying to rip him from the rope and swallow him.

He reached the end of the rope; rotten and torn. Below him, the pit narrowed, twisting and turning like the belly of a snake.

He clambered carefully onto the rocky wall. The sides of the pit were rugged enough for him to find natural handholds, but his arms were aching so much that tears came to his eyes. As he continued his arduous climb, he felt as though his soul was also descending into darkness. The surface seemed so far away, and his body was wracked by despair. He realised the true danger was not the risk of falling but the temptation to let go.

A feeling came upon him that even if he reached the bottom, the struggle to return to the surface would be too difficult to bear. He tried to push the thought out of his head.

Still, further down the tunnel, he slid. There were snakes slithering along the walls of the cavern, and another human skeleton, crouched against the wall, hands covering its face.

Darker it became, till he could barely see. Still, he struggled on. The path was illuminated by an iridescent glow that substituted for daylight.

He stopped and pressed his head against the wall. He was too tired to go on. The whispers had grown loud now, penetrating his skull. "Why," the voices said, "why go on? It's over. There's no going back."

After being trapped in this paralysed state for what seemed like hours, he summoned up what willpower he had left and continued the climb

He was starting to wonder if the pit was some kind of trick, an eternal trial that never ended. Maybe there was no bottom. Maybe the treasure was just a myth.

But then he remembered the day Grenn had found him and saved his life.

No. Grenn had survived the pit. Therefore, it was possible.

With renewed strength, Karl clawed his way down. Crawling, crawling, crawling for what seemed like hours on end.

Then suddenly, he saw it. No more rocks ahead, just a patch of dirt. He had reached the bottom.

His feet landed firmly on the ground.

He was expecting the place to be strewn with rubble, infested with snakes and spiders and littered with bones. But it was just a circle of dirt, the same size as the entrance to the pit.

But where was the treasure? He looked around. There was nothing.

Then he examined the walls more closely and saw a note jammed into one of the crevices.

He opened it and read. Then, he understood.

He started his climb back to the surface. Grenn sat on a log by the pit, making shapes in the soil with his walking stick. He heard the rope stretch and looked up to see it tighten. A smile touched the edge of his lips.

About an hour later, he heard the scrambling of feet on the rock. Karl emerged from the pit, and threw himself on the ground, breathing heavily.

Grenn stood up and approached him. He offered him a hand. Karl clasped it and rose to his feet.

"Do you understand what the gift is?" asked Grenn.

Karl nodded. "I think I do," he said.

"It's not gold or jewels," said Grenn, "it's far more precious than that." He paused for a moment, gauging Karl's reaction, then continued.

"It's the knowledge that you survived the pit," he said, "the certainty that comes with facing the deepest darkness and emerging alive. When the shadows enclosed you and the weight dragged you down, still, you pressed on. When hope seemed lost, and the surface a distant memory, still, you pressed on.

"And now, you have emerged from the pit, having faced down the demons that dwell within. If you can survive that, you can survive anything.

"This is what you now possess. This is the knowledge you take with you into the forest. The shadows cannot touch you when you have already faced worse and won.

"Go now, into the forest, and bring the light of your own rebirth. Bring redemption."

Karl thought about that for a moment. "How can there possibly be enough of us to save this world?"

"Everyone who survives brings light into the world," said Grenn, "one day, there will be enough of us to cleanse the land. However long it takes."

Karl thought about that, then nodded. "So is it time for me to leave?"

"There's no rush," said Grenn, smiling, "let us sit and talk awhile."

They sat down on the log, and Grenn spoke with Karl of what lay ahead.

Printed in the USA
CPSIA information can be obtained
at www.ICGtesting.com
LVHW091120221024
794498LV00007B/441